A.S. Dowidat

Sunday

Short Stories
in German and English

Parallel Text

Translated by
Timothy Phillips

Bibliographic information of the
Deutsche Nationalbibliothek:
The Deutsche Nationalbibliothek records this
publication in the Deutsche Nationalbibliografie;
detailed bibliographic data is available on the internet at
http://dnb.dnb.de.

Bibliografische Informationen der
Deutschen Nationalbibliothek:
Die Deutsche Nationalbibliothek verzeichnet diese
Publikation in der Deutschen Nationalbibliografie;
detaillierte bibliografische Daten sind im Internet über
http://dnb.dnb.de abrufbar.

Printing and Publishing / Herstellung und Verlag:
BoD – Books on Demand, Norderstedt
2nd Edition / 2. Auflage 2017

ISBN: 978-3-7448-1729-5

Das letzte Picknick

Bernd? Bernd, sag schon was! Soll ich noch mal reingehen? Ihr die Lippen feucht machen? Bernd?

Da geht er einfach an mir vorbei in die Küche und sagt kein Wort. Ich stehe auf, die Tür zum Schlafzimmer ist nur angelehnt. Im Zimmer ist es hell, Bernd hat die Vorhänge vor dem Fenster beiseitegeschoben. Eben ist er kurz auf dem Klo gewesen, dann ist er gleich wieder zu Biggi rein.

Sie sieht jetzt ganz friedlich aus, wie sie so daliegt. Ihr Mund ist leicht geöffnet. Ihre Augen sind geschlossen. Bernd kommt wieder ins Zimmer. Er setzt sich auf den Stuhl an Biggis Bett und blickt sie an. Zwischendurch wischt er sich mit der Hand über die Augen. Ich stehe nur da und weiß nicht, was ich sagen soll.

Biggi will unbedingt zu Hause sterben. Regelmäßig muss sie ins Krankenhaus zur Chemo, in den Tagen danach liegt sie zu Hause im Bett, weil sie so kaputt ist. Ich krepier' nicht im Krankenhaus, sagt sie immer. Lasst mich da nicht sterben! Ich will hier sein können, wenn's so weit ist. Bernd und ich sehen uns an. Wir können ihr diesen Wunsch nicht abschlagen, doch wir haben keine

The Last Picnic

Bernd? Bernd, say something! Should I go in again? Moisten her lips? Bernd?

He walks past me into the kitchen and doesn't utter a word. I get up. The door to the bedroom is ajar. In the room it's light, Bernd has drawn open the curtains to either side of the window. He's just been quickly to the loo and is now going back to Biggi.

She looks very peaceful the way she's lying there. Her mouth is slightly open. Her eyes are shut. Bernd comes back into the room. He sits down on the chair next to Biggi's bed and looks at her. Now and again he wipes his eyes with his hand. I just stand there and don't know what to say.

Biggi is determined to die at home. She has to go to hospital regularly for her chemo. In the days afterwards she lies in bed at home as she's feeling so bad. I ain't gonna kick it in hospital, she always says. Don't let me die there! When the time comes I wanna be here. Bernd and I look at each other. We can't deny her this wish but we've got no idea what it's going to be like.

Ahnung, wie das sein wird. Irgendwann holen wir sie aus dem Krankenhaus nach Hause, der Arzt schüttelt den Kopf. Sie wissen nicht, worauf Sie sich einlassen, haben Sie einen guten Hausarzt?

Dr. Grübner kommt jeden Tag, hängt einen neuen Beutel mit Flüssigkeit an und spritzt Morphium, davon wird Biggi etwas wirr im Kopf und manchmal sogar ganz lustig. Sie spricht davon, in welch tollem Hotel sie gelandet ist und fragt uns, wer der Direktor ist. In den letzten Tagen dämmert sie nur noch dahin. Bernd wechselt ihre Windeln, wir befeuchten ihr Lippen und Mund mit Wattestäbchen, legen ihre Lieblingsmusik auf, wechseln uns ab, bei ihr im Zimmer Wache zu halten, falls irgendetwas ist, sie vielleicht mehr Schmerzmittel braucht. Morgens geht Bernd runter und holt uns was zum Frühstücken aus dem Kühlschrank. Seit mehr als zwanzig Jahren betreibt er *Die Palette*, eine kleine Kneipe, darüber wohnt er mit Biggi in einer Zweizimmerwohnung.

Als er Biggi zum Sterben nach Hause holt, hängt er ein Schild an die Tür: Wegen familiärer Angelegenheiten geschlossen.

Zwischen Bernd und Biggi fliegen manchmal die Fetzen, Biggi zieht aus und kommt irgendwann wieder zurück, Bernd steht in der Zwischenzeit mit grimmigem Blick hinter dem Tresen

Eventually we fetch her from the hospital and bring her home. The doctor shakes his head. You don't know what you're letting yourselves in for.

Have you got a good family doctor?

Dr. Grübner comes every day, hangs up a new bag full of liquid and gives Biggi a morphium injection. This makes her somewhat mixed up in her head and sometimes she can be quite funny. She tells us how great the hotel is where she's staying and asks who the manager is. In the last few days all she's done is doze. Bernd changes her nappies, we moisten her lips and mouth with cotton buds, we put on her favourite music and we take turns in keeping watch, just in case something happens, maybe she needs more painkillers.

In the mornings, Bernd goes downstairs and fetches something out of the fridge for breakfast.

He's been running The Palette now for over twenty years. It's a small pub and he lives above it together with Biggi in a two room flat. When he brought Biggi home to die, he put a sign on the pub door: Closed for family reasons.

Occasionally Bernd and Biggi have a huge argument, Biggi moves out and comes back again sometime later. In the meantime Bernd stands behind the counter with a fierce look and bangs the beerglasses down on the counter.

und knallt jedem das Bierglas hin. Bei Bernd kann man nie sicher sein, ob er etwas im Scherz meint oder ernst. Mit Biggi bin ich zusammen zur Schule gegangen, irgendwann weiß Bernd auch, dass ich früher mal was mit Biggi gehabt habe, doch das war lange vor seiner Zeit.

Jetzt sitzen wir beide an ihrem Bett. Man muss wohl Dr. Grübner anrufen, damit er den Totenschein ausfüllen kann. Und den Bestatter, Spellmann, den Bernd gut kennt, er hat sein Geschäft um die Ecke, und ab und zu kommt er vorbei und gibt seinen Sargträgern einen aus.

Bernd?

Er sitzt da und blickt auf Biggi. Dann sieht er mich an, doch er sagt nichts.

Bernd, soll ich Dr. Grübner… oder Spellmann …?

Er sieht wieder auf Biggi.

Nee, warte, sagt er. Nicht so schnell. Ich habe der Biggi noch was versprochen.

Bernd kann auf mich zählen. Als Biggi zum Sterben nach Hause kommt und noch klar im Kopf ist, spricht sie öfter davon, wie gerne sie noch einmal am Flussufer wäre. Auf der Wiese sitzen, die Schiffe in der Nähe der Schleuse beobachten und in den Himmel blicken, wenn lang-

You can never tell with Bernd whether he's being serious or means something as a joke.

I went to school with Biggi. Bernd also found out that Biggi and I had been together, but that was ages before he appeared on the scene.

Now we're both sitting on her bed. We should call Dr. Grübner so he can issue the death certificate. As well as the undertaker, Spellmann, who Bernd knows well, his business is just around the corner and sometimes he drops in and buys a drink for his pall bearers.

Bernd?

He sits there and looks at Biggi. Then he looks at me but doesn't say anything.

Bernd, should I …you know, Dr Grübner or Spellmann?

He looks at Biggi again.

Nope. Wait, he says. Not so fast. I promised Biggi something.

Bernd can count on me. When Biggi came home to die but was still clear in her head, she often used to mention how much she'd like to go down to the river bank one more time. Sit on the grass, watch the boats by the lock and gaze at the sky as the sun slowly sets.

sam die Sonne versinkt. Montags, wenn die Palette geschlossen ist, haben wir ab und zu am Ufer in der Nähe der Brücke gegrillt. Einmal bin ich mit Bernd dort alleine gewesen, Biggi war wieder mal ausgezogen. Bernd zeigte mir einen Baum, an dessen Rückseite B & B 1992 eingeritzt ist.

Bernd?
Sag schon, was hast Du ihr versprochen?

Wir nehmen Bernds Wagen, einen alten Mercedes-Kombi. Es ist ein milder Spätsommertag, vielleicht besser so, dass es nicht mehr so warm ist. Bernd hat Biggi ihr Lieblingskleid angezogen, dazu die roten Schuhe, die er ihr zum letzten Geburtstag geschenkt hat. Bernd fährt den Wagen in den Hinterhof. Dann trägt er Biggi die Treppe herunter, sie wiegt ja kaum noch was. Doch ihr Gesicht sieht immer noch hübsch aus, auch wenn sich die Nase bereits spitz abzeichnet.

Bernd setzt sie auf den Rücksitz, ich setze mich neben sie, ihr Kopf lehnt am Türrahmen und Bernd deckt sie mit ihrem leichten Sommermantel zu. Während der Fahrt droht sie ein paarmal zur Seite zu kippen, ich rücke näher an sie heran, ihr Kopf fällt auf meine Schulter. Unterwegs hält Bernd an einer Tankstelle und besorgt ein paar

On Mondays, when The Palette was shut, we often had a barbecue on the river bank down by the bridge. On one occasion I was down there alone with Bernd. Once again Biggi had moved out. Bernd showed me a tree on which was scratched B & B 1992.

Bernd?
Tell me. What did you promise her?

We take Bernd's car, an old Merc estate. It's a mild, late summer's day, maybe it's just as well that it's not so warm. Bernd has dressed Biggi in her favourite dress and her red shoes which he gave her as a present on her last birthday. Bernd drives the car into the yard at the back. Then he carries Biggi down the stairs, she hardly weighs anything. And yet her face still looks pretty, even if the nose is already looking a little pointed.

Bernd puts her on the back seat. I sit next to her. Her head leans against the car door and Bernd covers her with a light summer coat. Whilst we're driving she threatens to flop over to the side. I push myself up closer to her and her head rests on my shoulder. On the way Bernd stops at a petrol station and buys a few beers and something to eat. I stay in the car with Biggi. It's busy

Flaschen Bier und etwas zu essen. Ich bleibe mit Biggi im Auto. An der Tankstelle ist viel los, ich bin froh, als Bernd endlich zurückkommt und mir eine volle Tüte nach hinten reicht.

Dann stecken wir mitten im Berufsverkehr fest, es geht nur noch schrittweise voran. Links schiebt sich ein Fiat vorbei, der Fahrer stiert geradeaus, auf der Rückbank sitzt ein kleiner Junge, der herüberblickt und anfängt, Grimassen zu schneiden. Ich strecke ihm die Zunge heraus und warte darauf, dass Biggi das ebenfalls macht.

Bernd lässt den Wagen auf der Wiese ausrollen, auf dem Uferpfad läuft ein Pärchen Hand in Hand, es beachtet uns nicht. Wir warten trotzdem, bis sie außer Sichtweite sind. Dann öffnet Bernd die Tür, steigt aus, öffnet die hintere Tür, hebt Biggi heraus und läuft mit ihr auf dem Arm zum Flussufer hin. Ich nehme die Tüte und gehe zum Kofferraum, öffne ihn und hole die Decken und die Klappstühle heraus. Kurz stutze ich, dann folge ich den beiden voll beladen.

Es ist etwas schwierig, Biggi auf den Klappstuhl zu setzen, sie kippt immer wieder zur Seite und droht dann, ganz herunterzurutschen.

Schließlich setzen wir uns so nah neben sie, dass wir ihren Rumpf mit unseren Schultern einklemmen. Biggis Kopf liegt auf Bernds Schulter.

at the petrol station. I'm happy when Bernd returns and hands me a full carrier bag.

Then we get stuck in the middle of the rush hour, we can only move forward at a snail's pace.

On our left a Fiat shoves itself forward, the driver staring straight ahead. A small boy is sitting on the back seat. He looks over towards us and starts to make faces. I stick my tongue out at him and wait for Biggi to do the same.

Bernd lets the car roll onto the grass. A couple is walking hand in hand along the path by the river. They don't see us. Nevertheless we still wait until they're out of sight. Then Bernd opens the door, gets out, opens the rear door, lifts Biggi out and carries her down to the river. I take the bag and go round to the boot, open it and take out the blankets and the deckchairs. I stop short for a moment, but then all loaded up I follow them both.

It's a bit difficult getting Biggi to sit on the deckchair, she keeps leaning over to one side and then threatens to slide off completely. In the end we sit so close to her that we jam her body between our shoulders. Biggi's head leans on Bernd's shoulder.

Ich öffne drei Flaschen Bier, dann erst fällt mir ein, wie unsinnig das ist. Ich reiche eine Flasche zu Bernd hinüber. Die dritte Flasche stelle ich auf den Boden neben Biggis Stuhl. Wir prosten ihr zu.

Für einen kurzen Moment überfällt mich das Gefühl, dass sie gleich aufwacht, nach der Bierflasche greift, und Überraschung! ruft.

Eine Weile sitzen wir schweigend da und blicken den Schiffen nach, die vorbeifahren.

Manchmal winkt jemand, und wir winken zurück. Als es kühler wird, legen wir uns die Decken über den Schoß. Bernd achtet darauf, dass auch Biggis Beine unter einem Stück Decke verschwinden. Der Himmel ist in ein glühendes Orange-Rot getaucht. Irgendwann bekommen wir Hunger und Bernd packt den Kartoffelsalat aus. Mit Plastikgabeln löffeln wir den Salat aus der Schale.

Kannst Du sie mal halten? Bernd rutscht auf seinem Stuhl nach vorne, ich lege meinen Arm um Biggi. Sie fühlt sich komisch an, kurz erschrecke ich, dann fällt mir etwas ein, an das offenbar keiner von uns gedacht hat, wir haben da ja keine Erfahrung. Bernd steht auf und geht zu der Baumreihe, die das Ufer säumt. Nach einer Weile kommt er zurück, ich sehe noch, wie er sein Messer wieder in der Hosentasche verstaut.

I open three bottles of beer before I realise how stupid that is. I hand one bottle over to Bernd. I put the third bottle on the ground next to Biggi's deckchair. We say cheers.

For a brief moment I had the feeling she would suddenly wake up, pick up the bottle of beer and shout "Surprise!".

We sit there for a while in silence and watch the boats sail past. Occasionally someone waves and we wave back. When it gets a bit cooler we cover ourselves with the blanket. Bernd makes sure that Biggi's legs disappear under the blanket too. The sky has been dowsed in a glowing orangey red. After a while we start getting hungry and Bernd opens the potato salad. We eat it straight out of the container with plastic spoons.

Could you hold her for a moment? Bernd pushes himself forward on his chair and I put my arm around Biggi. She feels strange. At first I'm a little shocked and then I realise something which clearly neither of us had thought of. We don't have any experience of this sort of thing. Bernd gets up and walks to the row of trees that run along the river bank. After a while he comes back. I notice him putting his knife back in his trouser pocket.

Wird langsam kalt, sagt er.

Du meinst, wir sollten wieder? Mhhm, ich glaub nur …, fühl mal Biggis Arm. Der Arm lässt sich kaum noch bewegen.

Bernd kratzt sich am Hinterkopf. Dann grinst er. So blöd, wie wir sind. Sie hätte sich totgelacht.

Es ist klar, dass wir sie jetzt nicht mehr so einfach auf die Rückbank setzen können. Und in den Kofferraum will Bernd sie auf keinen Fall legen.

Wir haben keine Ahnung, wie lange es dauern wird, bis die Starre sich wieder löst. Schließlich holt Bernd sein Smartphone heraus und googelt.

Gott im Himmel, ruft er. Das kann noch zwei Tage so bleiben. Er blickt mich an.

Mensch, Biggi. Jetzt auch noch das.

In der Nacht liege ich lange wach. Bernd hat mich gebeten, ihn noch eine Weile mit Biggi alleine zu lassen. Dann wollte er versuchen, sie irgendwie auf die Rückbank zu legen und mit einer Decke zuzudecken. Als ich mit der Straßenbahn über die Brücke gefahren bin, habe ich noch einmal zum Fluss hinab gesehen. Da saßen sie und von Weitem sah es so aus, als blickten sie gemeinsam aufs Wasser.

Getting a bit nippy, he says.

D'you think we should go back? Mhm, I think… try Biggi's arm. We could hardly move her arm.

Bernd scratched the back of his head. Then he grinned. We're so stupid. She'd have laughed her head off.

It's obvious that we can no longer simply sit her on the back seat. And there's no way that Bernd is going to put her in the boot. We've no idea how long it takes before the rigor mortis starts to fade. After a while Bernd gets out his smartphone and googles it.

Christ! he exclaims. She can stay like that for two days. He stares at me.

Damn you, Biggi. Anything else?

During the night I lie awake. Bernd asked me to leave him alone for a while with Biggi. Later he wanted to try to lie her down somehow on the back seat and cover her with a blanket.

As I rode over the bridge in the tram I looked down towards the river one more time. There they were sitting together, and from a distance it looked as though together they were gazing at the water.

Drei Tage später ist die Beerdigung. Es regnet, und als sich der Sarg in die Erde senkt, habe ich den Eindruck, dass Bernd vor sich hin grinst. Er hat mir nie gesagt, was er ihr eigentlich genau versprochen hat. Doch hat Biggi nicht einmal wie im Scherz gesagt, man solle sie nahe am Fluss begraben, mit Blick auf die Schleuse?

The funeral takes place three days later. It's raining and as the coffin is being lowered into the grave I have the feeling Bernd is grinning to himself. He's never told me exactly what he'd promised her. But didn't Biggi once say jokingly that she wanted to be buried down by the river with a view of the lock?

Meine Großmutter fuhr Motorrad

Mir fallen die alten Fotos ein. Auf einem von ihnen steht meine Großmutter vor der Schänke am Brückenkopf. Mütze und Motorradbrille auf dem Kopf, lacht sie in die Kamera. Sie trägt einen langen hellen Mantel, darunter Hosen mit engem Saum, flache Sportschuhe.

Auf einem anderen Foto mein Großvater. Er lehnt am Motorrad, mit kurzer Jacke und schweren Stiefeln, auf dem Kopf die Lederkappe. Das Motorrad hat einen gefederten Sitz und ist mit dem Hinterrad aufgebockt. Da waren wir oft, hat mir meine Großmutter einmal erzählt, jeden Sonntag ging's über die Brücke, vorher ein kleiner Zwischenstopp, dann weiter, manchmal bis Holland und wieder zurück. Irgendwo wurde Picknick gemacht auf einer Wiese, da hatten wir schon den Seitenwagen, erzählte sie, als sie mir das Foto zeigte, auf dem sie gerade ein Ei pellt. Mein Großvater sitzt neben ihr und beißt in ein Butterbrot. Das hat die Hanny fotografiert, die Hanny und der Max hatten auch schon Seitenwagen, erklärte mir Großmutter. Die Hanny und den Max habe ich nie kennen gelernt und Großmutter ist auch schon lange tot.

My Grandmother Drove a Motorcycle

I remember the old photos. On one of them my grandmother is standing outside the pub at the end of the bridge. With cap and goggles she's laughing into the camera. She's wearing a long, light-coloured coat, beneath it narrow trousers and flat shoes.

My grandfather's in another photo. He's wearing a short jacket, heavy boots and a leather cap and is leaning against a motorbike. The motorbike has a sprung seat and the rear wheel is jacked up on a stand. We often went there, my grandmother once told me, we went across the bridge every Sunday, took a short break and then we rode on, sometimes as far as Holland and back. We had a picnic in a field somewhere. We already had the sidecar then, she recounted as she showed me a photo of her peeling an egg. My grandfather is sitting next to her, biting into a sandwich. Hanny took this one. Hanny and Max already had a sidecar, my grandmother explained. I never met Hanny or Max and my grandmother has been dead for some time.

Ich komme nicht weiter. Nicht so. Wir schweigen. Vor uns die Biergläser sind wie Barrikaden aufgebaut. Beide sind noch fast voll. Seit einer Stunde sitzen wir hier. Und schweigen mehr, als dass wir reden würden. Ich wollte reden, unbedingt. Ein Gespräch führen, das klären soll. Was soll das bringen, hat Thorsten gesagt. Ich will so nicht weiter, habe ich nur gedacht und den Ort vorgeschlagen. Hinter mir steht eine alte Stechuhr. Über Thorsten hängen ein Grubentelefon und eine Spitzhacke an der Wand. Ich mag diesen Ort und seine Einrichtung. Vielleicht erinnert er mich an früher, als ich noch nicht lebte.

Mein Großvater war Bergmann, aber erst später, im Krieg. Davor war er jahrelang arbeitslos.

Da lud er sein Schifferklavier auf das Motorrad, packte meine Großmutter in den Seitenwagen, und dann fuhren sie über die Brücke auf die Dörfer. Er spielte für ein paar Pfennige in Kneipen, meine Großmutter musste aufpassen, dass er nicht zu viel trank, wie hätten sie sonst zurückkommen sollen. Mein Großvater musste aufpassen, dass die Arbeitsverwaltung nichts mitbekommt, sonst hätte sie die Unterstützung gestrichen, sie fuhren immer weiter hinaus, dort kannte sie niemand. Auch auf den Fotos aus dieser Zeit lacht meine Großmutter in die Kamera.

I'm not getting anywhere. Not like this. We sit in silence. The beer glasses stand in front of us like a barricade. They're both still nearly full. We've been sitting here for an hour. And we've been silent for longer than we've spoken. I wanted to talk. Desperately. Have a talk to clarify things. What's the point? Thorsten asked. I can't carry on like this, is all I'd thought and had suggested this place. Behind me there's an old clocking-in machine. Hanging on the wall behind Thorsten there's a telephone and a pick from the mine. I like this place and the way it's decorated.

Perhaps it reminds me of the past before I was alive. My grandfather was a miner, but only later during the war. Before that he'd been unemployed for years. He used to load his accordion onto the motorbike, put my grandmother into the sidecar and then drive them both over the bridge to the surrounding villages. He played for a few pennies in the pubs and my grandmother had to make sure that he didn't drink too much. Otherwise how would they get back home? My grandfather had to make sure that the labour office didn't catch on, if so they would have taken away his benefits. They drove out further and further so no-one recognized them. In the photos taken during this time my grandmother is laughing into

Was willst du denn?, fragt mich Thorsten.

Weiß ich das? Ich weiß, dass ich so nicht weiter will, so im Unverbindlichen. Thorsten besucht mich, fährt über die Brücke, die nach dem Krieg wieder aufgebaut wurde, bleibt über Nacht, ich besuche Thorsten, fahre über die Brücke, die heute einen anderen Namen hat, bleibe über Nacht, Begrüßungsküsse, Abschiedsküsse, bis zum nächsten Mal. Seit sechs Monaten geht das so. Für Thorstens Familie existiere ich überhaupt nicht, er spricht nicht von mir. Was soll ich sagen, wer du bist, hat er gesagt, ich will keine Beziehung.

Thorsten ist nicht der Typ für das Klassische, Ehe, Familie, Kinder, irgendwann ein eigenes Häuschen. Das wusste ich. Was wollte ich eigentlich von ihm? Vielleicht weiß ich das nicht mehr genau. Das alkoholfreie Bier schmeckt schal, ich trinke es in kleinen Schlucken.

Sie habe ihn sich einfach geangelt, hat meine Großmutter einmal erzählt. Hat ihn einfach gefragt, ob sie mal mitkommen könnte auf eine Tour. Dann saß sie hinten auf dem Motorrad und ist nicht mehr abgestiegen. Drei Wochen später wurde Verlobung gefeiert, ein halbes Jahr später die Hochzeit. Irgendwann konnten sie sich den Seitenwagen kaufen, da saß sie dann nicht mehr nur hinter ihm.

the camera too.

What do you want then? Thorsten asks.

Do I know? I know that I don't want to carry on like this, uncommitted. Thorsten visits me, rides over the bridge which was rebuilt after the war, stays overnight; I visit Thorsten, ride over the bridge which nowadays has another name, stay overnight; kisses on arrival, kisses on leaving, see you next time. It's been going on like this for six months. For Thorsten's family I just don't exist. He's never talked about me. Who should I say you are, he said, I don't want a relationship.

Thorsten is not the type for a traditional relationship, marriage, family, children, sometime a house of one's own. I knew that. What did I really want from him? Perhaps I don't know exactly. The non-alcoholic beer tastes flat, I sip it.

I simply picked him up, my grandmother once told me. I just asked him if I could go with him on a bike tour. Then she sat behind him on his motorbike and never got off again. The engagement party was three weeks later and half a year later the wedding. After a while they were able to buy the sidecar and she no longer had to sit behind him.

Er hat ihr gezeigt, wie man Motorrad fährt, sie hat es ausprobiert. Zuerst auf einsamen Feldwegen außerhalb der Stadt, früh am Morgen. Dann nahm sie Fahrunterricht, aber sie fiel durch die Prüfung. Ich war wohl zu nervös, erzählte sie lachend, aber was soll's, Hauptsache, ich konnte fahren. Für alle Fälle, erklärte sie mir verschmitzt, besser, ich fahre ohne bestandene Prüfung als Großvater, der zu viel getrunken hat.

Einmal musste ich dann tatsächlich fahren, sagte sie.

Noch eins? fragt der Kellner, der an unserem Tisch vorbeikommt. Ich nicke. Thorsten kippt das halbe Glas herunter, dann nickt er auch. Du weißt, dass ich mich nicht binden will, aber ich lasse dir alle Freiheiten, sagt Thorsten. Und was mache ich damit?, frage ich mich.

Thorsten gefiel mir, seine weiche Stimme, seine schlanken Hände, wie er sich beim Tanzen bewegte. Wir lachten uns zu, dann standen wir zusammen bei den Getränken, er goss mir das Glas voll und mir gefiel, dass er das Bier nicht aus der Flasche, sondern ebenfalls aus dem Glas trank. Wir saßen auf einem roten Sofa bei einem Kollegen, tranken Bier und unterhielten uns fast die halbe Nacht über alles Mögliche.

He showed her how to drive a motorbike. She tried it out. At first early in the mornings on lonely tracks across the fields outside the town. Then she took driving lessons but failed the test. I was too nervous, she said laughing. But it didn't matter, the main thing was that I could drive. Just in case, she explained mischievously. It's better I drive without having passed my test than grandfather when he's had too much to drink.

On one occasion I really did have to drive, she said.

One more? asks the barkeeper as he passes our table. I nod. Thorsten downs his remaining half and nods too. You know I don't want to get tied down and I let you have all the freedom you want, says Thorsten. And what do I do with it? I ask myself.

I liked Thorsten, his soft voice, his slender hands, the way he danced. We laughed and then we found ourselves standing next to each other by the drinks. He poured me a glass and I liked the way he drank his beer out of a glass and not out of a bottle. We sat together on a red sofa at a colleague's house, drank beer and stayed up half the night talking about life and the universe.

Großvater hatte zu viel getrunken, erzählte sie, er hatte in irgendeiner Dorfkneipe gespielt, es war spät geworden, aber wir hatten ganz ordentlich verdient. Der Wirt war großzügig, wenn Großvater spielte, wurden die Leute lustig und tranken mehr. Leider auch Großvater, dem der Wirt immer wieder ein neues Bier hinstellte. Es wurde später und später und er konnte unmöglich noch fahren. Da habe ich mir gesagt, Lisbeth, du kannst genauso gut fahren, hier weiß schließlich keiner, dass du keinen Führerschein hast, erzählte Großmutter. Also habe ich Großvater in den Seitenwagen verfrachtet, der Wirt lachte, er sagte, gut dass Sie fahren können, eine Frau und eine so schwere Maschine, alle Achtung. Das Schifferklavier wurde hinten auf dem Gepäckträger festgebunden und los ging's.

Ich fühle mich zu nichts verpflichtet, meint Thorsten, das habe ich dir von Anfang an gesagt.

Ich weiß, sage ich. Dann schweigen wir wieder.

Ich rief Thorsten drei Tage nach der Party an, wir verabredeten uns in der Stadt, ich fuhr über die Brücke, auf der anderen Seite an dem Brückenturm vorbei, wo früher die Schänke war und Großvater das Motorrad aufgebockt hatte.

Grandfather had drunk too much, she said. He'd played in some village pub somewhere, it had got late, but we'd done quite well. The pub owner was generous. When grandfather played people started enjoying themselves and drank more. Unfortunately grandfather did too and the pub owner kept giving him another beer. It got later and later and there was no way he could drive. That's when I said to myself, Lisbeth, you can drive just as well. Here no-one knows that you don't have a driving licence, recounted grandmother. So I loaded grandfather into the sidecar. The pub owner laughed. He said, "Good that you can drive. A woman and such a heavy machine! Amazing!" The accordion was tied to the luggage rack at the back and off we went.

I don't feel under any obligation, utters Thorsten, I told you that right from the beginning.

I know, I say. Then we fall silent again.

I called Thorsten three days after the party. We arranged to meet in town. I drove over the bridge to the other side, past the tower at the end of the bridge where the pub was and where grandfather had jacked up the bike.

Wir bummelten durch die Stadt, dann bekam ich Hunger und zog Thorsten in die Kneipe, in der wir jetzt sitzen. Danach gingen wir zu ihm und ich fuhr erst am nächsten Tag wieder über die Brücke zurück. Ich glaube, ich wollte ihn mir angeln. Ich nippe am Bierglas, mit der Zunge lecke ich mir den Schaum von den Lippen. Was mache ich mit meiner Freiheit, über die Brücke zu fahren, wann ich will, frage ich mich. Ich weiß, dass Thorsten nicht mit mir zusammenziehen will, dass er wohl überhaupt mit keiner Frau zusammenziehen würde. Das funktioniert für mich nicht, hat er mal gesagt, ich bin zu eigen, ich brauche meinen eigenen Rhythmus. Als der Kellner eben kam, wollte ich ihn eigentlich fragen, wie er sich das weiter vorstellt. Ich will keine Freiheiten, die ich nicht brauche.

Ich fuhr mit Großvater durch die Nacht, erzählte Großmutter. Er war eingeschlafen und schnarchte, das konnte ich sogar durch das Motorengeknatter hören. Und ich lenkte das Motorrad über die Landstraße. Erst nicht besonders schnell, aber auch nicht zu langsam, das hätte ja auffallen können. Großmutter grinste, wenn sie das erzählte.

Erst saß ich kerzengerade und steif auf der Maschine, dann beugte ich mich über den Lenker wie

We walked through the town and then I got hungry and dragged Thorsten into the pub where we're sitting now. Then we went to his place and I only drove back over the bridge again the following day. I think I just wanted to pick him up. I sip at the beer and lick the foam from my lips with my tongue. What am I doing with my freedom, driving over the bridge when I want, I ask myself.

I know that Thorsten doesn't want to move in with me, that he'll never move in with any woman. It doesn't work for me, he once said, I'm too unconventional, I need my own pace. Just when the barkeeper came I wanted to ask him how he imagined that would work in future. I don't want any freedom that I don't need.

I drove through the night with grandfather, said grandmother. He had fallen asleep and was snoring. I could even hear him above the noise of the engine. And I drove along the country roads. Not too fast at first, but not too slow as someone may have noticed. Grandmother grinned whilst she told me that.

When we set off I sat on the bike all stiff and upright, but eventually I bent over the handlebars and drove faster like a racer.

eine Rennfahrerin und fuhr schneller. Das machte richtig Spaß. Gut, dass Großvater davon nichts mitbekam. Es war eine sternklare Nacht und als wir über die Brücke fuhren, sah ich den leuchtenden Vollmond, erzählte Großmutter. Da musste ich plötzlich laut lachen und konnte nicht mehr aufhören. Ich fuhr juchzend und lachend über die Brücke und Großvater schnarchte immer noch im Seitenwagen. Und zu schnell fuhr ich auch.

Immer wenn Großmutter das erzählte, dachte ich, wie glücklich muss sie mit Großvater gewesen sein.

Ich habe das zweite Glas Bier ausgetrunken. Irgendwie bringt das hier nichts, denke ich. Eigentlich weiß ich, dass ich mit Thorsten nicht weiterkomme. Nicht so weiterkomme, wie ich es mir wünschen würde. Überhaupt mit einem Mann wünschen würde. Dass Thorsten dafür nicht der Richtige ist, wusste ich eigentlich von Anfang an.

Ich habe jetzt große Lust, über die Brücke zu fahren. Lass uns zahlen, sage ich zu Thorsten. Er blickt etwas überrascht, er hat noch gar nicht ausgetrunken. Kommst du noch mit? fragt er mich.

Ich glaube, heute nicht, sage ich. Das ‚heute' ist mir so rausgerutscht, das hätte ich weglassen können.

It was great fun. Good that grandfather didn't know anything about it. It was a clear night and as we drove over the bridge I looked up at the bright full moon, recounted my grandmother. All of a sudden I started to laugh out loud and couldn't stop. I drove over the bridge shrieking with delight and all the time grandfather was asleep in the sidecar. And I was driving too fast, too.

Whenever grandmother told me this story I always thought how happy she must have been with grandfather.

I've finished the second beer. Somehow I'm thinking this isn't getting anywhere. In fact I know that I'm not going to get any further with Thorsten. Not get any further as I would like to, with any man. Actually, I've known right from the beginning that Thorsten's not the right one. What I really want to do now is drive over the bridge.

Let's pay, I say to Thorsten. He seems somewhat surprised, he hasn't finished his drink yet.

Are you still coming with me? he asks. I don't think so. Not today, I say. "Today" just slipped out. I could have left it. We pay and get up. My motorbike is outside. Another goodbye kiss, see you then, yes, see you.

Wir zahlen, stehen auf, draußen steht mein Motorrad. Ein Abschiedskuss noch, bis dann, ja, bis dann.

Ich fahre durch die Stadt, dann bin ich endlich auf der Brücke, ich drehe den Kopf und sehe den Vollmond, der am Himmel über den grün leuchtenden Schornsteinen der Stadtwerke hängt. Auf einmal muss ich laut lachen und kann nicht mehr aufhören.

I drive through the town. Then at last I'm at the bridge. I look up and see a full moon hanging in the sky over the chimneys of the local factory lit up in green. All of a sudden I start laughing out loud and can't stop.

Buizid

Gestern Morgen ging ich zur Arbeit.

Ich zog meinen Mantel an, ließ mich die Treppe herunterfallen, auf der Straße sprang ich vor ein Auto, warf mich dann vor der Straßenbahn auf die Gleise, rannte gegen die Mauern des Arbeitshauses, schob meine Finger in das Zeiterfassungsgerät – es schrie – , auf den Knien kroch ich die Treppe zu meinem Zimmer hinauf, mein Kopf schlug die Tür auf, die Aktenregale fielen auf mich herab, mit meinem rechten Zeigefinger bohrte ich in der Steckdose herum, mittags saß ich in der Kantine in einem Topf kochenden Wassers, am Nachmittag lochte ich meine rechte Hand und heftete sie ab, schließlich sprang ich aus dem Fenster im vierten Stock und ging wieder nach Hause.

Nichts blieb übrig von mir an diesem Tag.

Heute bleibe ich zu Hause.

Officide

Yesterday morning I went to work.

I put on my coat and fell downstairs. Out on the street I jumped in front of a car. I threw myself on the track in front of an oncoming tram, ran against the walls of the workhouse, pushed my fingers into the clocking-in machine (it screamed), crawled on my knees upstairs to my office, banged the door open with my head, the shelves full of files fell on top of me, I bored with my right index finger into the socket on the wall, at lunchtime I sat in the canteen in a pot of boiling water, in the afternoon I punched holes in my right hand and filed it away, and finally I jumped out of the window on the fourth floor and went back home.

At the end of the day there was nothing left of me.

Today I'll stay at home.

Am Nachmittag

Wenn Farner seinen Rasenmäher aus der Garage fährt, sitzt Bergmann schon auf dem Bock. Dann umkreisen sie ihre Grundstücke, die Maschinen kreischen, und Farner und Bergmann blicken angespannt auf das Gras.

Neulich gab es ein kleines Unglück. Ein Stein musste sich in Farners Maschinenmessern verkrallt haben, dann wurde er hochgeschleudert und traf ihn am Kopf. Blutend sank Farner zusammen, während Bergmann noch eine Runde drehte, seinen Mäher in die Garage zurückfuhr und im Haus verschwand.

Es war dann ganz wunderbar ruhig.

Afternoons

When Farner drives his garden tractor out of the garage, Bergmann is already driving his own. They circle around their respective grounds, the machinery screeching away, with Farner and Bergmann looking intensely at the cut grass.

Recently there was a slight mishap. A stone must have got stuck in the blades. It was thrown up in the air and struck Farner on the head. Blood started to run down his face and Farner collapsed into his seat. Bergmann went round once more before driving his lawn mower back into the garage and disappearing into the house.

And then it was so wonderfully quiet.

Hühnchens Rache

Er wusste, dass irgendwann seine Stunde kommen würde. Er wusste dies und wartete darauf mit der Beharrlichkeit eines Elefanten, der irgendwann nur den rechten Huf zu heben braucht, um seinen vor ihm gestolperten Gegner darunter zu zerquetschen. Oberamtsrat Hühnchen konnte warten. Sieben Jahre hatte er auf die Beförderung vom Regierungsamtmann zum Amtsrat gewartet, zehn Jahre auf die Beförderung vom Amtsrat zum Oberamtsrat. Und nur drei Jahre musste er warten, bis er seine Schmähung rächen konnte.

Hätte der Minister nicht diesen süffisanten Unterton in der Stimme gehabt, wäre es vielleicht gar nicht so weit gekommen. Wegen einer völligen Nichtigkeit hatte der ihm die einzig seinen Fähigkeiten entsprechende Beförderung in den Höheren Dienst vermasselt. Dabei war er in den Augen Hühnchens selbst dumm wie Bohnenstroh.

Hühnchen hatte in den Vermerken an das Ministerbüro darauf bestanden, den Satz nach einem Doppelpunkt in Kleinschreibung weiterzuführen.

Dies hatte der Minister regelmäßig mit wütendroten Bemerkungen zur Rechtschreibung sanktioniert. Nur deshalb konnte Hühnchen bei diesem

Hühnchen's Revenge[1]

He knew his hour of glory would come. He knew it. And so he waited for it, like an elephant which only needs to lift its right foot to squash an adversary that has stumbled in front of it.

Oberamtsrat[2] Hühnchen could wait. He'd waited seven years to be promoted from Regierungsamtmann to Amtsrat, and then ten years from Amtsrat to Oberamtsrat. And now he'd had to wait three years to avenge his injustice.

If the minister hadn't had this smug undertone in his voice it may not have come to this. Thanks to nothing more than a triviality he had obstructed his promotion to the top level of the service, into the only job that matched his skills. And so in Hühnchen's eyes the minister was as thick as two very short planks.

In his memos to the minister's office, Hühnchen had always insisted on placing an apostrophe - when appropriate - after a plural noun that ended in s, as in two weeks' time. The minister had regularly commented on this in thick red ink with angry observations about the rules of punctuation.

in Ungnade gefallen sein. Dass er bei der letzten Beurteilungsrunde im Hause so schlecht abschnitt, konnte er daher nur dem Minister zu verdanken haben. Der ihn – das bestärkte seine Vermutung – bei der ersten persönlichen Rücksprache danach mit „Na Hühnchen, da war wohl alles Flattern umsonst" begrüßt hatte.

Nichts war umsonst, wenn man Warten konnte. Warten konnte bis zu der Stunde, in der man das Ego des Gegners zu Atomen pulverisieren würde.

Diese Stunde hatte vor drei Minuten begonnen. Eineinhalb Stunden dauerte der Empfang beim Verband der Toilettenartikelhersteller bereits, der Minister war ohne Unterbrechung von der vierstündigen Kabinettssitzung angereist, Hühnchen im Schlepptau, die Aktentasche unterm Arm, Taschentücher und Textmarker bereithaltend für die möglichen Bedürfnisse des Ministers. Der hatte eben das Angebot eines Kellners, der zu Anfang kleine Häppchen reichte, mit dem Hinweis auf seine Diät abgelehnt. Und dann, vor aller Augen, nach der Gurke auf Hühnchens Brötchen gegrabscht. Dabei nuschelnd, so etwas dürfe er essen. Und getrunken hatte er. Zwei Gläser Weißwein bereits und dazu reichlich Wasser.

This was the only reason why Hühnchen could have fallen out of favour. It must have been due to the minister that in the latest round of staff appraisals he had received such a poor report.

The same minister who – and this reinforced his speculation – at their subsequent meeting greeted him with, "So Hühnchen, there really was no need to get into such a flap, was there?"

Nothing is without reason if you are prepared to wait; wait until exactly the right moment to reduce your adversary's ego to a pile of atoms.

This moment had just arrived, three minutes ago. Coming straight from a four-hour cabinet meeting, the minister had subsequently joined the reception at the Association of Manufacturers of Toiletry Requisites and this had now been going on for a good hour and a half. Hühnchen was in tow with briefcase under his arm, tissues and highlighters at the ready should the minister require them. The minister had just refused a canapé offered to him by a waiter, referring to his diet as an excuse. And then, in front of everybody present, had grabbed a slice of cucumber off Hühnchen's open sandwich murmuring that he was allowed only to eat such things. And he'd already had a drink: two glasses of white wine as well as ample water.

Und seit drei Minuten war klar, dass Hühnchens Stunde gekommen war. Der Minister war unruhig geworden und hatte sich suchend umgeblickt. Der Präsident des Verbandes der Toilettenartikelhersteller deutete den Blick sofort richtig und beschrieb den Weg. Aus der Halle heraus, den Gang rechts herunter und dann die zweite Tür links. Schwache Blase, dachte Hühnchen triumphierend. Er wartete einen Augenblick, dann ging auch er los, den beschriebenen Weg entlang.

Er kam gerade noch rechtzeitig, der Minister befand sich in Startposition am Pissoir ganz hinten rechts. Hühnchen stellte sich daneben, nickte dem Minister aufmunternd zu und begann seinen Vernichtungsfeldzug.

Monatelang hatte er geübt, in den finstersten Spelunken hatte er nie die Kabine benutzt, sondern sich direkt neben die schmutzigsten Typen gestellt und sich so sämtliche Hemmungen abtrainiert. Er wusste, dass auch der Minister nie die Kabine benutzte. Keiner hätte es gewagt, ihm an diesem Ort zu folgen. Eine solche Annäherung bedeutete an sich schon fast Majestätsbeleidigung.

Der Minister wirkte verwirrt. Warf Hühnchen einen Blick zu, der von oben herab wirken sollte, dessen Wirkung er aber schon im Ansatz verfehl-

And for the last three minutes it had become clear to Hühnchen that his moment had arrived.

The minister had grown fidgety and was looking around the room impatiently. The Chairman of the Association of Manufacturers of Toiletry Requisites had immediately understood the situation and described the way. Go straight out of the hall, turn right, down the corridor and it's the second door on the left. A weak bladder thought Hühnchen triumphantly. He waited a moment and then he followed the same directions. He arrived at just the right time: the minister had assumed his starting position at the pissoir at the far end on the right. Hühnchen stood next to him, nodded briefly and encouragingly to the minister and then started his campaign of total annihilation.

He'd been practising for months. In the dingiest drinking holes he hadn't locked himself away in the toilet but had stood right next to the grimiest of men, and had thus trained himself to lose his inhibitions. He knew that the minister always used the pissoir. No-one would ever have dared to follow him into this of all locations. Such proximity was in itself an insult of almost majestic proportions.

te. Hühnchen konzentrierte sich längst auf anderes. Nach dem Ratschen des Reißverschlusses brauchte er nur zwei Sekunden, um einen triumphalen Strom sprudeln zu lassen. Nun war er es, der den Minister begleitend zur Geräuschkulisse von schräg unten ansah.

Der Minister starrte an die Toilettenwand, seine Gesichtsfarbe verdunkelte sich, seine Züge wurden starr. Das sah nach äußerster Konzentration aus, in die hinein Hühnchen den Blick sehr bedeutsam weiter nach unten schweifen ließ. Und dann ein süffisantes „Mhm" von sich gab, das sollte klingen wie: na, das wird wohl heute nichts mehr. Dann blickte er wieder geradeaus, leise vor sich hin lächelnd. Er schaffte dreiundzwanzig Sekunden, bis der letzte Tropfen versiegte. Der Minister neben ihm schaffte nichts.

Hühnchen hätte jetzt am liebsten gebrüllt wie ein Löwe. Stattdessen zog er den Reißverschluss wieder hoch, nickte dem Minister lächelnd zu und sagte den Satz. Er wusste, dass dieser Satz ihn endgültig erledigen würde. Es war ohnehin klar, dass er nach dieser Schmähung nie wieder an seinem Schreibtisch, sondern höchstens noch in der Materialausgabe landen würde. Diese Perspektive machte ihm jedoch nichts aus, er hatte dort seine Laufbahn begonnen.

The minister appeared confused. He glanced at Hühnchen with the intended effect of looking down from on high, but which from the outset was doomed to failure. Hühnchen was already concentrating on other matters. Having zipped open his trousers he only needed a couple of seconds before a triumphant stream began to pour forth. Now it was he, accompanied by the appropriate sound effects, who looked down at the minister.

The minister stared at the toilet wall, his face darkened and his features stiffened. He seemed to have sunk into complete and utter concentration whilst very pointedly Hühnchen allowed himself to look downwards. And then came a smug "Hm" intended to indicate, "Well, I guess that's it for today." Smiling quietly to himself he looked straight ahead again. He managed 23 seconds until the last drop trickled out. Next to him the minister had produced nothing.

Above all Hühnchen would have loved to have roared like a lion. Instead he zipped himself up, nodded smilingly at the minister and said it. He knew that this would finish him off completely. It was already evident that after this abuse he would never sit at his desk again but would be banned to the stationery store, if he was lucky.

Für die letzten Jahre genügte ihm dieser Rückzugsraum, dort würde er hin und wieder einen Plausch halten mit Kollegen, die wegen Druckerpapier, Kugelschreibern, Textmarkern und dergleichen vorbeikämen. In der Zwischenzeit hätte er Zeit genug, Gedichte zu schreiben.

Der Satz hing im Raum. Er hing über dem Minister wie eine dunkle Wolke, die sich langsam aufgetürmt hatte und der man den Blitz ansah, der sich aus ihr entladen hatte. Hühnchen hatte lange über diesen Satz nachgedacht. Er hatte ihn zu Hause vor dem Spiegel ausprobiert, in verschiedenen Versionen, mit unterschiedlichen Tonlagen, bis er die richtige gefunden hatte.

„Ein kleines Drama, nicht? Na, Ministerchen, da war wohl alle Konzentration umsonst." Er hatte diesen Satz so gesagt, als sei er ihm gerade erst eingefallen, doch den süffisanten Unterton hatte er lange geübt, bis er genau die Tonlage des Ministers traf.

Der starrte jetzt ins Nirgendwo hinter Hühnchen, die Kieferknochen mahlend.

Hühnchen straffte sich, atmete noch einmal tief durch und verließ den Ort gemessenen Schrittes. Auf dem Rückweg traf er den Präsidenten des Verbandes der Toilettenartikelhersteller, der sich über den Verbleib des Ministers wunderte.

He felt at ease with this future prospect as that was where he had started his career. Such a safe retreat would be suitable for his remaining years.

He would have occasional chats with colleagues who came to collect printer paper, ballpoint pens, highlighters and the like. And in the meantime he could dedicate enough time to writing poetry.

It hung in the air. It hung over the minister like a black cloud which had slowly built up and then suddenly let loose a bolt of pent-up lightning.

Hühnchen had thought about it for a long time. He'd practised it at home in front of the mirror in a number of variations and in a range of differing tones until he'd found just the right one.

"Having a little difficulty? Dear Minister, there really is no need to concentrate so hard, is there?"

He uttered this sentence as if he'd just thought of it. But he'd been practising the complacent tone for many hours until he could fully match that of the minister. The minister stared into space behind Hühnchen, grinding his teeth.

Hühnchen straightened, breathed in deeply and left at the appropriate, considered pace. On the way back he met the President of the Association of Manufacturers of Toilet Requisites who was wondering where the minister had got to.

Man nickte sich kurz zu, Hühnchen ging zum mittlerweile eröffneten Buffet und lud sich den Teller mit Geflügelsalat voll.

They nodded to each other. In the meantime the buffet had opened and Hühnchen piled his plate full with chicken salad.

[1]*Hühnchen: a) small chicken   b) term of endearment for a chicken*

[2]*The German federal civil service has a strict hierarchical structure reflected in its job title as below in descending hierarchical order:*

> *Oberamtsrat*
> *Amtsrat*
> *Regierungsamtmann*

Sonntag

Der Alte war schon den ganzen Tag im Haus herumgelaufen. Im Wohnzimmer immer um den großen Tisch herum, als wolle er Karussell spielen, die Treppe wieder hinauf, stand auf dem Absatz, machte kehrt, ging die Treppe wieder hinunter, dann wieder hinauf, als könne er nur durch dieses wiederholte Hinauf- und Hinabsteigen eine Ordnung wiederherstellen, die ihm schon lange verlorengegangen war.

Ihn nervte das, er konnte das nicht ertragen, das mit ansehen zu müssen, immer auch die Angst, der könnte dann auf der Treppe stolpern, fallen, unten aufschlagen, und dann wäre alles vorbei. Vielleicht dachte er auch das, es müsste ihn erschrecken, wenn er das dächte. Er rief nach seiner Frau, sie solle doch endlich herunterkommen, sich kümmern, die Vase auf dem Tisch würde der gleich umstoßen, es ist doch nicht mein Vater, rief er.

Nach einer Weile kam sie herunter, ging in die Küche, er hörte den Wasserhahn, dann das Klappern von Geschirr, der Alte lief um den Tisch herum, immer um den Tisch herum, er selbst hatte sich auf den Sessel am Regal gesetzt, der Ab-

Sunday

The old man had been walking around the house all day. Round around the large table in the living room as if playing on a roundabout. Repeatedly up the stairs to the landing where he turned round and back down again, as though this constant repetition was the only way he could restore a routine which had deserted him a long time ago.

It got on his nerves. He couldn't bear having to watch him do this, constantly fearing that he might trip up on one of the stairs, fall and thud all the way back down. And then it would be all over.

Perhaps he only thought this as having such thoughts ought to shock him. He called out to his wife. It's about time she came down, looked after him, he was about to knock over the vase on the table, after all it's not my father, he shouted up.

After a while she came down, went in the kitchen and he heard her turn on the tap followed by a clatter of plates. The old man kept running around the table, always around the table. He had positioned himself slightly apart in the armchair by the bookshelf, in the pit box, he thought, I'm sitting in the pit box.

seits stand, in der Boxengasse, dachte er, ich sitze in der Boxengasse.

Dann kam sie, sie trug einen kleinen Teller, auf dem lagen ein Apfel und das Obstmesser, nahm den Alten am Arm, führte ihn zum Sofa, komm, sagte sie, setz dich, für heute ist es genug. Dann saß er auf dem Sofa, wippte unruhig hin und her, sie legte ihm die Hand auf die Schulter, komm sagte sie, ich schneide dir einen Apfel auf, Vitamine brauchst du. Sie schälte den Apfel, schnitt ihn in dünne Scheiben, er wippte und sah irgendwohin, wo etwas war, das nur er sah.

Warum sitzt du dahinten, rief sie herüber, er fühlte sich gestört, er hatte alles wie in einem Film beobachtet, er brauchte diese Distanz, die in einem Wohnzimmer gerade noch möglich war. Er wollte nicht den Sabber sehen, der dem Alten in dünnen Fäden aus dem rechten Mundwinkel hing.

Ich kann den Film einlegen, sagte sie, aber es war keine Aufforderung, etwas dazu zu sagen, sie machte es sowieso, egal, was er dazu gesagt hätte.

Er blieb in seiner Ecke, sie stellte den Teller, den sie auf ihrem Schoß gehabt hatte, auf den Tisch zurück, stand auf, machte den Schrank auf, holte die Kassette heraus und schob sie in den Videorekorder. Der Alte beobachtete sie, sein Wippen war ruhiger geworden, jetzt schaukelte er

Then she came in. She was carrying a small plate with an apple and a fruit knife. She took the old man by the arm and led him to the sofa. Come, she said, sit down, that's enough for today. He sat down on the sofa, rocking uneasily backwards and forwards. She put a hand on his shoulder. Come on, she said, I'll slice you an apple, you need some vitamins. She peeled the apple and cut it into thin pieces. He carried on seesawing and looked at something which only he could see.

Why are you sitting back there? she called over to him. He felt as if he'd been disturbed, he'd been watching everything as if in a film. He needed this distance which was still just about possible in the living room. He didn't want to see the drool that was hanging in thin threads out of the right hand corner of the old man's mouth.

I can put the film on, she said, but it wasn't an invitation to be responded to, she did it anyway regardless of what he might have said. He remained in his corner. She put the plate that had been on her lap back on the table, stood up, opened the cabinet, picked out the cassette and pushed it into the videorecorder. The old man watched her, his seesawing had grown calmer. He was now slowly rocking just the upper part of his

seinen Oberkörper langsam hin und her und sah ihr zu. Sie setzte sich wieder, nahm die Fernbedienung vom Tisch, drückte den Knopf, sofort waren Stimmen zu hören, der Film war nicht ganz zurückgespult gewesen, der Alte saß jetzt ganz still, wenn das nur immer so wäre, dachte er in seiner Ecke. Aus den Lautsprechern hörte er die Stimme des Alten, er lachte, und eine Frauenstimme, beide lachten, er konnte auch aus seiner Ecke sehen, wie fröhlich sie gewesen sein mussten. Und dann ist sie weggestorben und hat ihn uns überlassen, dachte er voll Bitterkeit, dabei war sie viel jünger gewesen als er, sie hätte ihn pflegen können. Er sah zu seiner Frau, sie hatte wieder den Teller mit den Apfelscheiben auf dem Schoß, sie nahm eine, führte sie zum Mund des Alten, willst du auch, rief sie herüber, als ob sie nicht wüsste, dass er nichts essen könnte, solange der Alte sabbernd am Tisch saß, die eine Hälfte der Scheibe hing aus seinem Mund, langsam, sagte sie und schob sie vorsichtig weiter hinein. Er sah den Alten kauen, wie in Zeitlupe, und meinte das Schmatzen bis in seine Ecke zu hören.

Das konnte er am wenigsten ertragen, die Geräusche, sie hätte den Film lauter machen sollen, aber er traute sich nicht, das zu sagen. Er wäre jetzt am liebsten hinausgegangen, aber er blieb in

body backwards and forwards and was looking at her. She sat down again, picked up the remote control from the table and pushed the button.

Suddenly there were voices, the film hadn't been completely rewound. The old man sat completely still. If only it could always be like that, he thought in his corner. He heard the old man's voice coming from the loudspeakers, laughing, and a woman's voice, both were laughing. He could see from his corner how happy they must have been. And then she died and left him to us, he thought, full of bitterness. She was much younger than he was, she could have looked after him. He looked at his wife. She'd put the plate with the slices of apple back on her lap, took one and held it towards the old man's mouth. Do you want some too, she asked across the room as if she didn't know that he couldn't eat anything so long as the old man was sitting at the table, drooling, with one half of the apple slice hanging out of his mouth. Slowly, she said, and carefully pushed it further in. He saw the old man chewing, as if in slow-motion, and imagined he could hear his slobbering all the way back to his corner.

That's what he could bear least of all, the noises. She could have turned up the volume of the film but he didn't dare say anything.

seiner Ecke, nahm die Zeitung, die auf dem Boden lag, schlug sie auf und verschwand dahinter.

Dann hörte das Schmatzen auf, er hörte nur noch die Stimmen aus den Lautsprechern, als wäre sie noch da, dachte er, als wäre sie noch da und der Alte würde mit ihr lachen und Scherze machen, als wäre er noch da, noch richtig da, dachte er. Dann hörte er, dass jemand vom Sofa aufstand, aber er blickte nicht auf, ein langsames Schlurfen über den Teppich, das konnte nur der Alte sein, jetzt fängt er wieder an herumzulaufen, dachte er. Als das Schlurfen unvermittelt aufhörte, blickte er doch auf, schlug die Zeitung zur Seite und sah den Alten vor dem Fernseher stehen. Er stand gebückt, die Windel beulte die Hose aus, die er trug, er hatte eine Apfelscheibe in der Hand und drückte sie gegen den Bildschirm des Fernsehers.

Er sah das und konnte nichts sagen, seine Frau stand auf und ging langsam zu dem Alten hin und blieb hinter ihm stehen. Der drückte immer noch die Apfelscheibe gegen den Bildschirm, er hörte das Lachen aus den Lautsprechern, sie lachen miteinander wie zwei Verliebte, dachte er und dachte, der Fernseher war teuer, dann hörte er, wie der Alte schluchzte, und sah, wie seine Schultern zuckten.

Most of all he would have loved to have left, but he stayed in his corner, picked up the newspaper which was lying on the floor, opened it and disappeared behind it.

Then the slobbering stopped. He could only hear the voices issuing from the speakers, as if she was still there, he thought, as if she was still there and the old man was laughing with her, joking around as if he was still there, still really there, he thought. Then he heard someone get up from the sofa but he didn't look up, a long shuffle across the carpet. That could only be the old man, now he's going to start walking around again, he thought. When the shuffling suddenly stopped he looked up, put the newspaper to one side and saw the old man standing in front of the television. He had bent forwards, the nappy he was wearing caused the seat of his trousers to bulge out, he had a slice of apple in his hand and was pressing it against the television screen.

He saw it and yet he couldn't say anything. His wife stood up, slowly went over to the old man and hovered behind him. He was still pressing the slice of apple against the screen. He heard the laughing coming out of the speakers, they`re laughing together like two lovers, he thought and remembered that the television was expensive.

Die Hand des Alten, in der er die Apfelscheibe hielt, glitt am Bildschirm herab, er fingerte mit der anderen Hand hinterher, dann hatte er etwas gefunden, knapp unter dem Bildschirm war die Klappe des Rekorders, er drückte dagegen.

Das war teuer, dachte er in seiner Ecke, so ein Kombigerät, und wenn eins kaputt ist, kann man das andere auch nicht mehr gebrauchen. Aber er konnte nichts sagen, und dann sah er, wie der Alte die Apfelscheibe, die sehr dünn geschnitten war, in den Schlitz unter der Klappe schob, bis zur Hälfte, dann blieb sie stecken. Der Alte schüttelte sich, kehlige Geräusche kamen aus seinem Mund, als ob er lachen wollte, dachte er in seiner Ecke, dann sah er, wie der Alte sich umwandte und ihn anblickte oder an ihm vorbeiblickte und sah seine Augen, die hell waren und sah sein Gesicht, das vor Freude verzerrt war.

Da schlug er die Zeitung wieder zurück, als wollte er sich verstecken, und fing an zu lesen.

Then he heard the old man sobbing and saw his shoulders trembling. The old man's hand which was holding the slice of apple slid down the TV screen. He fumbled around with the other hand and then he had found something. The flap of the videorecorder was right under the screen and he pressed against it.

It's expensive, he thought in his corner, a combined TV and video set and when one of them's broken you can't do anything with the other one. But he couldn't say anything, and then he watched as the old man pushed a slice of apple which had been cut very thinly into the gap under the flap until it was half way in and got stuck. The old man shook himself, deep throaty noises were coming out of his mouth as though he wanted to laugh, he thought in his corner. Then he saw the old man turn round and look at him, or look beyond him, and saw how bright his eyes were and how his whole face was contorted by pure joy.

He threw open the newspaper again, as if he wanted to hide, and began to read.

A.S. Dowidat

was born in Duisburg, Germany, in 1970. She grew up in the Rhineland and studied Protestant theology and law. She has worked as a newspaper delivery girl, a gatekeeper at a psychiatric hospital, an administrative lawyer, vicar and hospital chaplain.

Timothy Phillips

was born in Tavistock, England, in 1959. He grew up in Hereford, studied French, German and Music, and has worked as a language trainer, manager, a freelance translator and in publishing.